Books by Julia Donaldson

This book belongs to

I celebrated World Book Day 2017
with this gift from my local bookseller,
Macmillan Children's Books,
Julia Donaldson and Lydia Monks.

This book has been specially produced to celebrate 20 years of World Book Day. For further information, visit **www.worldbookday.com**.

World Book Day in the UK and Ireland is made possible by generous sponsorship from National Book Tokens, participating publishers, authors, illustrators and booksellers.

Booksellers who accept the £1* World Book Day Book Token bear the full cost of redeeming it.

World Book Day, **World Book Night** and **Quick Reads** are annual initiatives designed to encourage everyone in the UK and Ireland – whatever your age – to read more and discover the joy of books and reading for pleasure.

World Book Night is a celebration of books and reading for adults and teens on 23 April, which sees book gifting and celebrations in thousands of communities around the country: **www. worldbooknight.org**

Quick Reads provides brilliant short new books by bestselling authors to engage adults in reading: **www.quickreads.org.uk**

*€1.50 in Ireland

JULIA DONALDSON

Princess Mirror-Belle

and Snow White

#WorldBookDay20
FREE BOOK
with your World Book Day token

WORLD
BOOK
DAY
20
2 MARCH 2017

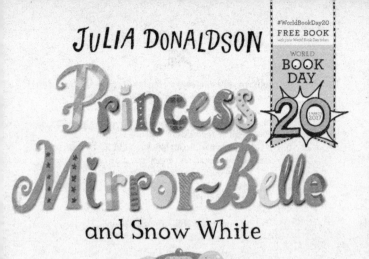

Illustrated by

LYDIA MONKS

MACMILLAN CHILDREN'S BOOKS

This story first published 2003 and 2015 as 'Snow White and the Eight Dwarfs'
in *Princess Mirror-Belle* by Macmillan Children's Books

This edition published 2017 by Macmillan Children's Books
an imprint of Pan Macmillan
20 New Wharf Road, London N1 9RR
Associated companies throughout the world
www.panmacmillan.com

ISBN 978-1-5098-4086-1

1 3 5 7 9 8 6 4 2

A CIP catalogue record for this book is available from the British Library.

Printed and bound by CPI Group (UK) Ltd, Croydon CR0 4YY

Princess Mirror-Belle and Snow White

Ellen's big brother Luke was singing again.

"Seven little hats on seven little heads. Seven little pillows on seven little beds," he sang, standing on a ladder and dabbing paint on to the branches of a canvas tree. A blob of paint landed on Ellen's hand. She was squatting on the stage, painting the tree trunk.

Ellen sighed heavily – more

because of the song than the blob of paint. Luke had been singing the seven dwarfs' song almost non-stop ever since he'd joined the local drama group and got a part in the Christmas pantomime.

"Seven pairs of trousers on fourteen little legs," he sang now.

"No one could call *your* legs little," said Ellen. "You should be acting a giant, not a dwarf."

"There aren't any giants in *Snow*

White, dumbo," said Luke. "Anyway, I told you, we all walk about on our knees."

"So that Sally Hart can pat you on the head," said Ellen. She knew that Luke was keen on Sally Hart. In fact, she guessed that he was only in the pantomime because Sally was acting Snow White.

Luke blushed but all he said was, "Shut up or I won't get you a ticket for tonight."

The first performance of *Snow White* was that evening, and at the last minute the director had decided that the forest needed a couple of extra trees. Luke had volunteered to go and paint them, and Mum had persuaded him to take Ellen along.

Although Ellen was too shy to want to be in the play, it was fun being in the theatre in front of all the rows of empty seats. But Luke wouldn't let her have a go on the ladder, and soon she had painted the bottom of the two tree trunks.

Luke was getting quite carried away with the leaves and acorns, still singing the annoying song all the time. He didn't seem to notice when Ellen wandered off to explore the theatre. She opened

a door in a narrow passageway behind the stage.

The room was dark and Ellen switched on the light – or rather, the lights: there was a whole row of mirrors. This must be one of the dressing rooms.

Some beards were hanging up on a row of hooks. Ellen guessed they belonged to the seven dwarfs. She unhooked one and tried it on. It was quite tickly.

"Seven little beards on seven little chins," she sang into a mirror.

"And seven mouldy cauliflowers in seven smelly bins," her reflection sang back at her.

But of course it wasn't her

reflection. It was Princess Mirror-Belle.

Quickly, Ellen turned her back, hoping that Mirror-Belle would stay in the mirror. Mirror-Belle was the last person she wanted to see just now. Their adventures together always seemed to land Ellen in trouble.

But it was too late. Mirror-Belle

had climbed out of the mirror and
was tapping Ellen on the shoulder.

"Let's have a look at your beard,"
she said, and then, as Ellen turned
round, "I'd shave it off if I were
you – it doesn't suit you."

"It's only a play one," said Ellen.
"Anyway, you've got one too."

"I know." Mirror-Belle sighed.

"The hairdresser said the wrong spell and I ended up with a beard instead of short hair."

"Couldn't the hairdresser use scissors instead of spells?" asked Ellen.

"Good heavens no," said Mirror-Belle. "An ordinary one could, maybe, but this is the *palace* hairdresser we're talking about."

She turned to a rail of costumes, pulled a robin outfit off its hanger and held it up against herself.

"Put that back!" cried Ellen, and then, "You'll get it all painty!"

They both looked at Mirror-Belle's left hand, which had paint on it, just like Ellen's right one.

"Have you been painting trees too?" Ellen asked.

"No, of course not." Mirror-Belle looked thoughtful as she hung the robin costume back on the rail. Then, "No – trees have been painting *me*," she said.

Ellen couldn't help laughing. "How can they do *that*?" she asked.

"Not *all* trees can do it," replied Mirror-Belle. "Just the ones in the magic forest. They bend down their branches and dip them into the muddy lake and paint anyone who comes past."

"How strange," said Ellen.

"I don't think it's so strange as people painting trees, which is what

you say you've been doing," said
Mirror-Belle.

"They're not real trees," Ellen
explained. "They're for a play."

Mirror-Belle looked quite
interested. "Can I help?" she asked.

"No, you certainly can't," said
Ellen, horrified, but Mirror-Belle
wasn't put off.

"What sort of
trees are they?"
she asked. "I'm
very good at
painting bananas.
And pineapples."

"Pineapples don't
grow on trees, and
anyway—" but Ellen

broke off because she heard the stage door bang.

"Ellen! Where are you?" came Luke's voice.

"I'm coming!" Ellen yelled. Then she hissed to Mirror-Belle, "Get back into the mirror! Don't mess about with the costumes! And *stay away from the trees*!"

That evening Ellen was back in the theatre, sitting in the audience next to Mum and Dad. *Snow White* was about to start.

Mum squeezed Ellen's hand. "You look nervous," she said. "Don't worry – I'm sure Luke will be fine."

But it wasn't Luke that Ellen was nervous about – it was Mirror-Belle. What had she been up to in the empty theatre all afternoon? Ellen was terrified that when the curtain went up, the trees would be covered in tropical fruit and the costumes would be covered in paint.

The curtain went up. There were

no bananas or pineapples to be seen. The forest looked beautiful. Dad leaned across Mum's seat and whispered, "Very well-painted trees, Ellen."

Sally Hart – or rather, Snow White – looked beautiful too, with  her black hair, big eyes and rosy cheeks. Over her arm she carried a basket, and she fed breadcrumbs to a chorus of hungry robins. None of them seemed to have paint on their costumes.

Ellen breathed a sigh of relief. Everything was all right after all! Mirror-Belle must have gone back into the dressing-room mirror.

A palace scene came next. When the wicked Queen looked into her magic mirror and asked, "Mirror, mirror on the wall, Who is the fairest one of all?" for an awful moment Ellen was afraid that Mirror-Belle might come leaping out of the mirror, shouting "I am!" But of course she could only do that if it was *Ellen* looking into the mirror. Stop being so jumpy, Ellen told herself – Mirror-Belle is safely back in her own world.

When the scene changed to the dwarfs' cottage, Mum gave Ellen a nudge. Soon Luke would be coming on stage!

And yes, now Snow White was asleep in one of the beds, and here came the dwarfs, shuffling in through the cottage door. Ellen knew that they were walking on their knees but the costumes were so good, with shoes stitched on to the front of the baggy trousers, that you couldn't really tell.

Luke was acting the bossiest dwarf – Typical, Ellen thought. He told the others to hang up their jackets and set the table. Then they started to dance around and sing the song that Ellen was so tired of hearing.

"Seven little jackets on seven little pegs. Seven little eggcups, and seven little eggs."

But something was wrong. One of the dwarfs was singing much louder than the others, and not getting all the words right. When the other dwarfs stopped singing and started to tap out the tune on the table, the dwarf with the loud voice carried on:

 17

"Seven stupid people who don't know how to count. Can't they see that seven is not the right amount?"

The audience laughed as they realised that there were *eight* dwarfs and not seven. But Ellen didn't laugh. Dwarf number eight had to be Mirror-Belle, and there was bound to be serious trouble ahead.

Up on the stage, Luke looked furious. He stopped tapping the table and started chasing Mirror-Belle round the room. He was trying to chase her out of the door but she kept dodging him as she carried on singing:

"Eight little spoons and eight little bowls. Sixteen little woolly socks with sixteen great big holes."

Ellen felt like shouting, or throwing something, or rushing on to the stage herself and dragging Mirror-Belle off. But that would just make things worse. All she could do was to watch in horror.

In the end, Luke gave up the chase. With one last glare at Mirror-

Belle he strode over to the bed where Snow White was sleeping. His cross expression changed to one of adoration when Snow White woke up and sang a song.

"Will you stay with us?" Luke begged her when the song had finished.

"Yes, do stay and look after us," said another dwarf.

"We need someone to comb our beards."

"And wash our clothes."

"And shine our shoes."

"And cook our meals."

"And clean our house."

All the dwarfs except Mirror-Belle were chiming in.

"There's nothing I'd like better!" exclaimed Snow White.

Mirror-Belle turned on her. "You must be joking," she said angrily. "You shouldn't be doing things like that – you're a *princess*! You should be bossing *them* about, not the other way round."

The audience laughed – except for Ellen – and Snow White's mouth fell open. Ellen felt sorry for her:

she obviously didn't know what to say. But Luke came to the rescue.

"Be quiet!" he ordered Mirror-Belle. "You don't know anything about princesses."

"Of course I do – I *am* one!" Mirror-Belle retorted. "I'm just in disguise as a dwarf. I thought Snow White might need some protection against that horrible Queen. I'm pretty sure she's going to be along soon with a tray of poisoned apples, and—"

"Shut up, you're spoiling the story!" hissed Luke, and put a hand over Mirror-Belle's mouth. Snow White looked at him in admiration. Luke made a sign to someone

offstage, and a second later the curtain came down. It was the end of the first half.

"Isn't Luke good?" said Mum in the interval. "He never told us he had such a big part."

"That little girl playing the extra dwarf is a hoot, isn't she?" said Dad. "She sounds a bit like you, Ellen. Who is she?"

"I don't know," muttered Ellen. It

was no use mentioning Mirror-Belle to her parents, who just thought she was an imaginary friend. Ellen licked her ice cream but she was too worried to enjoy it properly. What would Mirror-Belle get up to in the second half of the show?

The curtain went up again. Snow White was sweeping the dwarfs' cottage. Ellen was relieved that there was no sign of Mirror-Belle. She must have gone off to work with the other dwarfs.

The wicked Queen appeared at the cottage window. She looked quite different – like an old woman – as she held out a tray of apples and offered one to Snow White.

"The dwarfs made me promise not to buy anything from a stranger," said Snow White.

"There's no need to buy," replied the disguised Queen. "Just open the window, and I'll give you one!"

Snow White opened the window and took an apple in her hand. She still looked doubtful.

"Don't you trust me?" asked the Queen. "Look, I'll take a bite out of it myself first to prove that it's all right." She did this and handed the apple back to Snow White.

Snow White had just opened her mouth when a voice cried, "Stop!" and a second figure appeared at the cottage window. Oh no! It was Mirror-Belle.

"Stop! Don't you realise, she took that bite out of the green half of the apple. It's the red half that's poisoned!" she warned Snow White.

Snow White took no notice and was about to bite into the apple when Mirror-Belle snatched it from her. She snatched the tray of apples from the Queen too. The next moment she had burst in through the cottage door, pursued by the Queen.

Some steps led down from the stage into the audience, and Mirror-Belle ran down them. She ran through the audience, the Queen hot on her heels.

When Mirror-Belle reached Ellen's seat she whispered, "Here, take this!" and thrust the tray of apples on to Ellen's lap. Ellen didn't know what to do, but was saved from doing anything by the Queen, who snatched the tray back. Mirror-Belle grabbed it from her again and ran on.

Meanwhile, Snow White, who had run off the back of the stage, reappeared holding Luke's hand and followed by the other dwarfs. They joined in the chase, round and round the audience and back on to the stage. Luke overtook the others. He caught Mirror-Belle by the shoulders and shook her.

"Give back those apples!" he ordered.

"What! Do you *want* Snow White to be poisoned?" protested Mirror-Belle. "Some friend you are!"

"Who is she, anyway?" asked Snow White – except that she didn't sound like Snow White any more, she sounded like Sally Hart.

"I don't know but we'll soon find out!" said Luke – sounding like Luke and not a dwarf – and he ripped Mirror-Belle's beard off.

"Ellen, it's you!" he exclaimed.

"Oh no I'm not!" said Mirror-Belle. "Your sister Ellen is in the audience – there, look!" She pointed, and to Ellen's embarrassment not only Luke but everyone else on the stage and in the audience was looking at her.

Not for long, though. Soon all eyes were back on Mirror-Belle, who was throwing apples into the audience.

"Don't eat them, *and don't give them back*!" she ordered.

Just then a man in a suit came on to the stage. Ellen recognised him as Mr Turnbull, the director. He strode up to Mirror-Belle.

"I don't know who you are or where you come from, but you'd better go back there before I call the police!" he said.

"Don't worry, I will!" said Mirror-Belle. Mr Turnbull made a grab for her but she dodged him and ran out through the cottage door. Mr Turnbull and all the actors followed her, and Ellen heard the Queen shout, "Oh no! She's got my mirror now!"

A moment later, Mirror-Belle was climbing back into the cottage through the open window, clutching the Queen's mirror. She scuttled into the dwarfs' cupboard just as everyone else came charging back in through the door.

"Where is she?" asked Mr Turnbull, with his back to the cupboard. Mirror-Belle popped her head out.

"She's behind you!" yelled the audience. Mr Turnbull turned round but now the cupboard door was shut.

"Oh no she's not!" said Mr Turnbull.

"OH YES SHE IS!" the audience shouted back.

Snow White opened the cupboard door and peered in.

"Is she there?" asked Mr Turnbull.

"I don't think so," said Snow White. She picked up her broom

and swept around inside, just to
make sure. "What's this?" she
asked, as she swept an object out of
the cupboard.

"It's my magic mirror!" said the Queen. "So she must have been here."

"Well, she's gone now, thank goodness," said Mr Turnbull. He turned to face the audience.

"I'm sorry about all this, ladies and gentlemen," he said. "Anyone who wants their money back can ask at the box office. But now, on with the show!"

"Seven little cups and seven little plates," sang Mum next day, as she served up Ellen's lunch. Luke was having a lie-in.

"Oh, Mum, don't *you* start!"

"Sorry. Wasn't Luke brilliant last night? I can't wait to show him the piece in the paper."

"Let's have a look."

Mum passed Ellen the paper, and this is what she read:

"The Pinkerton Players' performance of *Snow White* last night was a comic triumph. The hilarious chase scene was hugely enjoyable, and so was the entertaining scene in which the director pretended to offer the audience their money back.

"All the cast gave excellent performances, especially Sally Hart as Snow White and Luke Page as the bossy dwarf, but the real star of the show was the child who played the Eighth Dwarf. Sadly, she was not present at the curtain call.

Perhaps she was too young to stay up so late.

"I have only one criticism of the show. Why did this child star's name not appear in the programme? Everyone wants to know who she is, and everyone wants to see more of her."

Yes, thought Ellen. Everyone except me.

About the Author

Julia Donaldson is one of the UK's most popular children's writers. Her award-winning books include *What the Ladybird Heard, The Snail and the Whale* and *The Gruffalo*. She has also written many children's plays and songs, and her sell-out shows based on her books and songs are a huge success. She was the Children's Laureate from 2011 to 2013, campaigning for libraries and for deaf children, and creating a website for teachers called picturebookplays.co.uk. Julia and her husband Malcolm divide their time between Sussex and Edinburgh. You can find out more about Julia at www.juliadonaldson.co.uk.

About the Illustrator

Lydia Monks studied Illustration at Kingston University, graduating in 1994 with a first-class degree. She is a former winner of the Smarties Bronze Award for *I Wish I Were a Dog* and has illustrated many books by Julia Donaldson. Her illustrations have been widely admired. You can find out more about Lydia at www.lydiamonks.com.

Also available

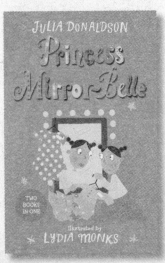

And coming soon

If you have enjoyed this story,
turn the page for an extract from
another book you might like.

TOM PERCIVAL

Little Legends

THE SPELL THIEF

Meet Jack and his talking chicken
Betsy, Red, Rapunzel, Hansel and
Gretel, and a host of other
Little Legends as they have
fantastic new adventures!

1

A Ship Comes In

*J*ack walked through the Deep Dark Woods with his pet hen Betsy tucked under one arm. He took a deep breath of the woodland air. It smelt fresh and exciting. Today was going to be a good day, he could just tell.

He walked towards a small wooden cottage surrounded by a neat wooden fence. There was a fountain in the garden, also made of wood, but instead of water, it was blowing sawdust high into the air.

'Whaaaat?' squawked Betsy.

'Don't worry, Betsy, it's only sawdust,' replied Jack. He wasn't surprised that his hen had just spoken to him. After all, Betsy was a magical hen. Sadly, 'What?' was the only thing she could say, which made most of their conversations rather one-sided.

WHAAT!!

Jack wiped his feet on the wooden door-mat and knocked on the door. He heard booming footsteps

4

from inside. The door swung open with a creak and a very woody smell.

A large man stood in the doorway, covered in wood shavings and holding a lopsided wooden cup.

'Well, look who it is!' he exclaimed with a smile. 'Come on through, Jack! Red and the others are all out back.'

He ushered Jack inside, where every surface, and in fact every *thing*, seemed to be made from wood . . . including the carpet and the curtains.

'So, how have you been, Jack?' asked Red's dad.

'Good, thanks,' replied Jack politely. 'How about you?'

'Oh, good, Jack, very good!' exclaimed Red's dad. 'In fact, I've just made a breakthrough!'

'A breakthrough?' asked Jack.

'With the wooden socks!' replied Red's dad.

'Don't you mean *woollen*?' countered Jack.

'Woollen socks?' repeated Red's father, as if it was the most ridiculous thing he'd ever heard, 'I'm a woodcutter Jack, not a *wool-cutter*!'

'Er, right . . .' said Jack.

'Do you want to try them on?' asked Red's father, holding out two very solid, very wooden-looking socks.

'Um, not right now,' replied Jack. 'I'd better go and catch up with Red. But thanks for the offer.'

———◆◆———

Jack raced through the house and into the garden. The tree house towered up in front of him. Red's dad had carved it out of one giant tree.

Jack's friends were all sitting in the main room when he climbed in.

'Morning, all!' he called out.

Red grinned, Rapunzel did her very best curtsy, and the twins waved enthusiastically.

PRIVAT!
CEEP OUT!

'Hey –' started Hansel.
'– Jack!' finished Gretel.
Hansel and Gretel often
finished each other's sentences.

Sometimes it could be confusing.

'Hey, Jack!' called Red. 'Do you want the good news or the bad news?'

'The good news?' asked Jack hesitantly.

'The good news . . .' said Rapunzel, leaving a long pause, 'is that there's a ship coming into town from Far Far Away!'

'Whaaat?!?!' squawked Betsy.

Jack gasped. A boat from Far Far Away! His dad might have sent him a letter . . .

'Yep!' added Red. 'It should be

arriving any minute! We're going to have a race up to Look Out Point to watch it come in – last one there is a smelly troll!'

'So what's the bad news?' asked Jack.

'The bad news is that Hansel's just tied your shoelaces together!' said Rapunzel as she and everyone else scrambled excitedly from the tree house.

Collect
them all!

Little Legends are
also available from

Me Books

B⊙⊙K IN FOR YOUR NEW ADVENTURE TODAY

CELEBRATING

WORLD **BOOK DAY**

20

2 MARCH 2017

3 brilliant ways to continue YOUR reading adventure

1 VISIT YOUR LOCAL BOOKSHOP

Your go-to destination for awesome reading recommendations and events with your favourite authors and illustrators.

 FIND YOUR LOCAL BOOKSHOP

Booksellers.org.uk/ bookshopsearch

2 JOIN YOUR LOCAL LIBRARY

Browse and borrow from a huge selection of books, get expert ideas of what to read next, and take part in wonderful family reading activities – all for FREE!

FIND YOUR LOCAL LIBRARY

Findalibrary.co.uk

3 DISCOVER A WORLD OF STORIES ONLINE

32 podcasts to try

Stuck for ideas of what to read next? Plug yourself in to our brilliant new podcast library! Sample a world of amazing books, brought to life by amazing storytellers. **worldbookday.com**

HAPPY BIRTHDAY WORLD BOOK DAY!

Let's celebrate . . .

Can you believe this year is our **20th birthday** – and thanks to you, as well as our amazing authors, illustrators, booksellers, librarians and teachers, there's SO much to celebrate!

Did you know that since WORLD BOOK DAY began in 1997, we've given away over **275 million book tokens**? WOW! We're delighted to have brought so many books directly into the hands of millions of children and young people just like you, with a gigantic assortment of fun activities and events and resources and quizzes and dressing-up and games too – we've even broken a **Guinness World Record**!

Whether you love discovering books that make you **laugh**, CRY, *hide under the covers* or **drive your imagination wild**, with WORLD BOOK DAY, there's always something for everyone to choose–as well as ideas for exciting new books to try at bookshops, libraries and schools everywhere.

And as a small charity, we couldn't do it without a lot of help from our friends in the publishing industry and our brilliant sponsor, NATIONAL BOOK TOKENS. Hip-hip hooray to them and three cheers to you, our readers and everyone else who has joined us over the last 20 years to make WORLD BOOK DAY happen.

Happy Birthday to us – and happy reading to you!

SPONSORED B

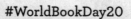

#WorldBookDay20